Midnight's Scream

A Strange Honeymoon

Sd Mikail

 pencil

ISBN 978-93-5458-287-5
© Sd Mikail 2021
Published in India 2021 by Pencil

A brand of
One Point Six Technologies Pvt. Ltd.
123, Building J2, Shram Seva Premises,
Wadala Truck Terminal, Wadala (E)
Mumbai 400037, Maharashtra, INDIA
E connect@thepencilapp.com
W www.thepencilapp.com

DISCLAIMER: *This is a work of fiction. Names, characters, places, events and incidents are the products of the author's imagination. The opinions expressed in this book do not seek to reflect the views of the Publisher.*

Author biography

Syed Mikail Ali was born on 4th January,1986 at GopalPur, Birbhum, West Bengal, in a lower middle class Muslim family. As family financial situation was not good, he completed BA Honours in English Literature from Krishna Chandra College under The University of Burdwan with a lot of difficulties. During his high school and college studies he had to work as a tuition teacher to feed his family and to maintain his own study cost. Situation became worst after his grandmother, Rokeya Bibi's death. She used to get a little pension and that was the family's assured income hardly enough for daily two meals. So he was bound to stop his studies to start an odd job. A rich man named Kazi Johir Alam from Dubrajpur supported him by providing financial help to complete his graduation. His childhood was not normal like other child. His mother was a prey of domestic violence in her in-law's house. She came back to her maternal home. So he was brought up in maternal grandmother's house. He had bitter experience of poverty from childhood. He had experienced different family problems and violence. After competing graduation in 2006, he was madly searching for a job. Although he was earning little money by offering tuition but the income was uncertain. Many poor students were taught by him who hardly were able to pay any fees. He started working as a teacher. He worked in different schools. In his 10 years teaching career he worked in different states in India. He closely observed different social issues in different states as he lived in multiple society of different social and cultural background. Being a teacher he was in touch with parents of different social, cultural and religious background. He has widely visited different states in India. Now he is teaching and staying in Maldives.

CONTENTS

5

Foreword

MIDNIGHT'S SCREAM

SYED MIKAIL ALI

All rights reserved by the Author

Preface

"By time, indeed mankind is in loss; except those who have believed and done righteous deeds and advised each other to truth and advised each other to patience" – Noble Quran (Surah-103, Al-Asr)

****

"Oh Mankind! Why thou cry for not having this or that? Did thou bring anything with you or will you take anything with you? Thou came empty hand and so shall thou return." – Bhagwat Geeta

****

"So we fix our eyes not on what is seen, but on what is unseen. For what is seen is temporary, but what is unseen is eternal" (-2 Corinthians 4.18)

****

Chapter - I

"Hello! Juber?"

"Yes. Speaking."

"Asalamo alaikum brother Juber. This is Aslam speaking"

"Walekum Salaam brother Aslam. Yes! What happened? How did you remember me so early in the morning? Has all guests gone? I enjoyed a lot in your sister's marriage yesterday. It was great."

"Just I received a call from my sister and she is crying a lot. She is calling us. Can you come with me? Actually my father and elder brother were very busy yesterday and slept late night as you know just her marriage was over. Now they are sleeping soundly."

"Yes I can come with you but what has happened to her. Is there any big problem? "

"I don't know. She is crying a lot. She is calling us. You please get ready fast. I am coming with my bike to your house. Be ready as soon as possible."

"Ok you come. I will be ready."

After eight minutes Aslam comes with his bike to Juber's house. They live in the same village. Yesterday Aslam's sister was married and they enjoyed a lot in the marriage party. Aslam's sister is married to a businessman who lives in a village 8 km away from this village. All family members had happily sent Sana (Aslam's sister) and gave a glorious see off when she left her native village and her own home forever to start a new life with an unknown person. Sana left her home and entered into a new world – her husband's home.

"What is the matter? Why is she crying? Did you ask her?"

"She is not saying anything. She called my brother, father, mother and sister many times but they all are sleeping soundly as they are very tired. Yesterday they were very busy and slept late night. I saw three miscalls in my phone from Sana and I called her back and she started crying a lot like a child."

"One day is not over in her in-laws' house. Problem started! O Allah! Please solve the problem. Allah please give her patience and power to overcome all difficulties."

Aslam rode the bike at a high speed and reached the house of his sister's in-laws'. There also the colour and excitement of marriage party was not over. All were in a happy mood. Loud Hindi music can be heard. Aslam and Juber met Sana who was alone in her bedroom. The room was well decorated with flowers but the decoration was torn here and there as seemed that the bride and the groom had a fight. The bed was in a bad condition and pillows were thrown here and there. As Aslam comes near his sister he was shocked. The dress of her sister was torn here and there; marks of brutal slapping can be seen on her face. Marks of stick were vividly seen on her hands. She was groaning in pain. She started sobbing.

"What had happened Sana?"

Only she was sobbing.

"Sana please tell us what has happened."

She keeps sobbing.

She was threatened so badly that she was not able to express her pain. Aslam comes close to her and sits beside her and keeps his hand on her back.

"Aaahhh!" Sana groans in pain. Aslam can see many bright brown marks of stick on her back. Her hair was not arranged. Her torn bra was on the bed. Dry drops of blood can be seen on her legs and on bed. Scratching wounds can be seen on her arms and throat. With great pain and difficulty she lift her cloth and showed her right thigh. It was totally brown – it was brutally beaten. On the thigh also he can see the dry drops of bloods. Tears come from Aslam's eyes and he also start crying –

"Why did he beat you like an animal?"

"He is an animal." Sana says sobbingly.

"Plesae take me to hospital."

"First let's talk to father."

"Father! He has married me to an animal. He does not receive my call in need. You all are animal. You all men are animal!"

'Sana please keep quiet. People will come to know the matter. It will be a big prestige issue for our family. Please have patience for the sake of Allah. I will take you to hospital. First let me talk to father"

Juber comes near who was also watching all these things and says -

"Really your brother-in-law is an animal. You must report the matter to the police. It is a case of marital rape. It is a crime. He must be punished."

"In marriage there is no rape. Sana must compromise. She must not say no to her husband. She has no right to say no." Angrily replied Aslam to Juber.

"Sana, nobody heard your scream at night?" – asks Juber to Sana.

"All were busy with music and dance whole night. Loud

bollywood Hindi music was going on and odd dance was in progress. They were all enjoying our marriage reception party. I was crying a lot – groaning in unbearable pain – screaming, but it was heard by none. Nobody came to rescue me. My so called husband cannot feel my pain – cannot hear my scream. Instead he tortures a lot. He beats me brutally like an animal. He is a very cruel and heartless man. Whether I am physically fine or not that does not matter to him – only my flesh matters. I don't know how you chose him for me."

Sana sobs in pain and her wet eyes wanted to tell many things but who will listen to her. Aslam informed the matter to his father. Aslam goes to meet his brother-in-law who was having breakfast with his friends and was in a jolly mood as they were having a lot of fun.

"Oh Brother Aslam! When did you come?"

"Asalamo alaikum brother. I came fifteen minutes before. I want to talk to you alone. Please come."

"Here all are my close friends – no need to hesitate to say anything or keep anything secret. You can tell me now."

"I want to take Sana to hospital. She is not feeling well. It is urgent."

"Brother Aslam you know well that all women experience that first night pain. I don't think it is necessary to take her to hospital. It is natural pain. She will be fine after sometimes. Don't worry. I will take care of her."

"No she is not fine. I think she must be taken to hospital. She is groaning in pain. She is having high fever also."

"Will you teach me? She is my wife. I am her husband. You don't have any right to take any decision regarding her. She is mine now. Whether she has to be taken to hospital or not I will decide. Whatever I deem fit I will do only."

"Why did you beat her so brutally brother?"

"I told you that she is now my wife. What I will do with her that I will decide. You don't poke your nose in our husband-wife matter. I can do anything with her because she is mine. I will beat her more if she says no again tonight."

"But brother you need to understand her problem also. She is having some problem."

"If she has any problems then keep her at your home. Did you understand?"

"Please brother try to understand the matter. Don't be so cruel. It is your responsibility to protect her and to take care of her."

"That I am doing well. You better keep your mouth shut now."

Aslam family members arrive. All are surprised. The matter was going to turn to be more grave. Aslam's brother-in-law becomes very angry when he sees his wife's family members coming to his house unexpectedly and shouts -

"She has called her family without my permission. I will teach her a lesson now in front of her parents and brothers. How did she dare to call them in my home without my permission?"

The newly married groom goes to beat the wounded bride again but is stopped by his family and friends. He starts abusing her. Sana's mother and sister go to Sana and talk to her.

Sana's father comes and asked her mother –

"What has happened?"

"Last night she was beaten brutally by our son-in-law."

"Beaten brutally by our son-in-law! But why?"

Sana's mother whispers at her father's ears -

"Sana's menstruation started yesterday evening. Whenever her period starts she becomes very ill because of heavy pain. She was having severe pain in her lower abdomen and fever also. She was not physically fit. Last night was her first night with her husband. She refused. So our son-in-law became very angry and beat her."

"Not only beat her brutally but also raped her." – said Sana's sister angrily.

Father remained silent for a moment and slapped Sana's Mom very badly in front of her children and said –

"You are a careless and useless woman! You don't know the dates of your daughter. When marriage date was fixed I asked you. You did not tell anything at that time. It is only your fault. Due to your fault Sana is suffering."

All become silent. Before this we could hear loud noise of Hindi bollywood song and children were shouting and dancing. Now everything is stopped. Sana's father goes to his son-in-law and says –

"Dear son-in-law it is our mistake. I apologize for the mistake. Please allow us to take her to hospital. Please forgive Sana."

"It's ok. You can take her to hospital."

They took Sana to the hospital. The lady doctor who was treating Sana says to Sana's elder brother –

"She has received serious injury. She needs to be admitted for treatment. I cannot permit her to go home after treatment keeping in mind her health condition."

"Ok. Admit her. But try to release her as soon as possible."

"How did this happen to her?" – the lady doctor asks the

elder brother.

"Nothing serious has happened. It is a case of domestic violence between husband and wife. It is not a big matter." - replies the brother.

"But she has received serious injuries. She is brutally beaten and raped during her period. She cannot sit or sleep properly because of pain. She is having high fever. She is breathing with difficulties. She is groaning in pain."

"You please treat her properly and cure her as soon as possible." – the brother replied the doctor harshly.

"But this is a crime – a great crime." – says the doctor.

Sana's father comes. The lady doctor says the same thing to him but he also gives the same reply -

"We know it is a big crime. But we are helpless. We have spent a lot of money for her marriage – around Rs 2000000 (twenty lakhs). We have no option other than compromising. We cannot do anything. We cannot take any action against our son-in-law. It is a minor family problem – we will solve it." – says Sana's father to the doctor casually.

"It is marital rape. It is a crime. You better take legal step now or else your daughter will suffer the same problem whole life. If you keep quiet now, your son-in-law will never mind doing the same crime again and again making her life a hell." – says the doctor.

"Doctor we can understand everything but we cannot do anything. Try to understand the matter. We must save the marriage at any cost. I have spent a lot of money for her marriage." – says the father.

As the nurse was treating Sana inside the chamber, Sana makes a lot of groaning painful sound – full of deep pain and agony. Suddenly she shouts at her brother and father –

"With whom have you married me? With an animal! You have thrown me to a wild animal who cannot understand my problem. He brutally uses my flesh to satisfy his thirst. My physical condition doesn't matter to him. What type of man have you chosen for me?"

The elder brother goes and slaps Sana – "Keep quiet. You must not say no to him. He is your husband. He has full right over you. If you had not refused, this problem would never have happened."

Sana sobs – "You all men are animals – wild animals."

The doctor shouts at the elder brother.

"You seemed to be a Muslim. I am a non-Muslim but I read the Noble Quran. I practise many noble things of Islam practically in my life and they can make our life and society much better and it can bring peace in family and society and in fact it can bring peace to the whole world. In Quran Allah has strictly forbidden man to approach woman during her periods. What kind of Muslim you are! You all are Muslim for name sake. Don't claim yourself to be Muslim while you cannot follow its noble practical things." – says the doctor.

"Excuse me madam. Don't teach me Quran. I know it very well. You please mind your business. You please do your duty. Please stop lecturing at us." – says the brother angrily and leaves the doctor's chamber.

"I apologize doctor for the misbehavior of my son. It is not his fault – it is my fault. I was very busy with my business and did not care for my children's proper education. Though I sent him to good schools to make him a modern man but never care to teach him Quran or other Islamic aspects. May be the same is the case with my son-in-law. To make him a modern man, his parents may have forgotten to teach him Quran and Islam like me."

"Papa I was screaming in pain whole night nobody was there to hear my plight. Nobody was there to rescue me. All the family members were busy in late night party. They were enjoying loud music and odd dance. I became a registered and legalized victim. He has threatened me that he will beat me more if I refuse again tonight. Please don't send me to that animal. Papa please save me from that animal."

Sana sobs in pain.......

"It is my fault Sana. I did not choose a man for you who can love you and take care of you. I was blind and proud with my wealth. I selected a wealthy person without knowing his character and behavior. I only judged and selected him based on his wealth. Forgive me Sana...... forgive me....."

Chapter - II

Juber narrated the whole incident of Sana to me in the afternoon. I felt extremely sorry for her. Tears rolled down from my eyes after listening the sad incident happened to her. I came home and sat on the chair in my small room. My mind became busy with my past. I became reminiscent. I remembered many life incidents with Sana, the sweet girl. I was in love with her. I know her well. She is a lovely, sweet and beautiful girl. We became very close friend when we were doing graduation in college. I know her from childhood. But our relation became deeper in college. She was very intelligent and good at studies. She helped me a lot to complete my projects and assignments. She was very cooperative. This is her fate! How bad luck she has! She is beaten and raped brutally by her husband! My mind was not able digest all these things happened to her. I still love her. I cannot believe the fact that she has refused her husband as personally I know her how sexy she is. I will never forget that afternoon when I had sex with her first time. How much curious she was about sex. It was a hot summer afternoon. We were coming home from college. We were very busy in completing our assignments as the submission deadline was very near. She had computer with internet connection. We can easily find many answers with the help of Google-Baba, the all-knower. Already we solved many assignments together in this way. I told her that I will come to her home in the evening to solve the assignments.

"But I will go to attend a marriage function in the evening. You better come now."

"Now it is not possible. I am feeling very hungry and thirsty. I can come after finishing my lunch."

"You can have lunch with me at my home. I may become busy for getting ready for the marriage party. I may have to go to Ruchi's Beauty Parlour. Please come now."

"I didn't deny the offer." She called me at her home and offered a nice lunch.

I had a nice lunch with her and a great time.

"Come to my room. I will start the computer and we can find the answers of the assignments."

"Yes let's go and do that."

When she entered her room she saw the room was not clean. She called one of the lady servant and said with smile -

"Aunty did you forget to clean my room?"

"No Madam. I was busy with cooking also. Badi Madam (Sana's mother) is not feeling well today. She gave me full responsibility of cooking meals for lunch."

"What has happened to mom?"

"Today her blood pressure has become high."

"How is mom now?"

"After taking medicine she is feeling well. She is having bad headache also. She is taking rest."

"Ok you clean it quickly. I will see mom."

"Please don't disturb her. She is sleeping now. Let her take rest."

"Ok. I will not talk to her. I will just go and see her."

I also went with Sana to see her mom. She was sleeping

soundly as if she had taken some sleeping pills. I was amazed to see the big rooms of the bungalow and very nice interior decorations made it more attractive and beautiful.

We came back to her room and it was clean. The servant switched on the AC and the room became cool very soon.

"Your mother's health is not fine."

"Here nobody's health is fine except me and Aslam. Some are having physical health problem and some are mental patient. Nobody cares for the family. These servants are better. They care for me more than my family members. In this family nobody has time for the family. All are busy in earning money – all of them want more and more money. I don't know when their thirst for money will be quenched"

"But we need money. Without money we cannot live."

"I know we need money. I don't think that without money we cannot live. I think we can better live without money."

"What are you saying Sana. We cannot imagine our life without money. Money is all. If you have money, you have everything."

"Not everything! May be something or many things but not everything! We cannot have everything with money."

"That's true. But who cares for that. The world is busy in earning more and more."

"Money was made as a servant to serve us – our society. But this servant has become master now – it's a dangerous master."

"Whatever may be but you people are having money and enjoying a nice life. Isn't it?"

"No! It is true that we are having money but not having life – at least not having a nice life. You may think we are living in a big bungalow but actually we are living in a concrete jungle. These well decorated rooms may look very attractive and beautiful. But the people who live here have ugly heart. It is only a house – not a home. Peace cannot reign here though luxury abounds."

"Why are saying so Sana. Be positive. People are suffering a lot due to lack of money. People are not getting proper food, medicine and shelter as they don't have money."

"When people have lot of money, it makes them patient also – it kills the humane in him. My family is a live example. My parents did a lot of hard work to earn money. Now you see they have money but it is useless for them."

"How money can be useless Sana? It is impossible."

"My father is a sugar and heart patient. He is also suffering from rheumatism. My mother is also suffering from BP problem, gas problem, severe back pain, often suffer from bad headache. They have developed different health hazards. They eat less food and more medicines. The doctor has forbidden them to eat many foods. Limited fruits they can eat. Only plain chapatti and plain vegetables with very less or without salt is their main menu in lunch and dinner. If they start eating food of their choice very soon they will be in big problem. Almost all tasty and delicious foods are forbidden for them. Now you tell me is their hard earned money useful for them. They have money but they don't dare to eat what their hearts long to eat. Now tell is their money useful for them."

"Yes you are correct. But who thinks so much. People are busy in earning and saving – not in spending. There is no guarantee of tomorrow but we are anxious of our future. We are giving a lot of emphasis for our future which is uncertain ignoring the precious present."

"Yes! The very thinking of future is destroying our present. To make a prosperous future we forget to enjoy our present. When that future comes we lose the ability or mentality to enjoy it. That's the irony of our life."

Sana became very emotional. She started saying something in different way –

"I have seen how dangerous money is. I will never forget that night. Still that midnight's scream rings in my ears – the helpless cry of Fatima, my sister-in-law. She was very lovely and loved us all and tried to make this concrete house a home. But she was burnt alive! And after that incident my mother became a patient forever. My younger sister got a deep shock from this incident and she also became a mental patient."

"What had happened that night? Why your sister-in-law was burnt alive? Who did this?"

"Five years ago! I was in grade 9. My elder brother Asraaf got married to Fatima. She was from a very good family. She will never go outside without her hijab in head. She used to offer five compulsory prayers, used to observe 30 days fasting during Ramzan, was kind with servants and treated them with respect. She alone used to take care of the whole family. She used to take special care of my parents. She was so lovely. Already her father gave a lot of gold, cash, furniture and a car to my brother as a gift or you can say as a dowry. But my brother was ever thirsty of money. He was trying his luck to become a famous politician and got full moral support from my father. He was often in need of more cash. He used to force Fatima to bring more cash from her father. She did it many times willingly and unwillingly. He had sold almost all of her gold ornaments. It was panchayat (local government) election time. He was in need of more money to win the election. He forced Fatima to bring more money from her father. But for the first time she came empty hand as her father was not able to arrange more cash. But my brother did not listen anything. He beaten her brutally and tried to force her to bring more cash. But she knew her father's condition. She refused. My brother burnt her alive in the kitchen that night. Nobody heard her scream. Aslam was in Delhi. I and my mother went to rescue her. She was screaming a lot as she was engulfed by fire and her scream pierced my heart. We covered her with a blanket and extinguished the fire. She got severe burn injury. She was groaning in burnt pain like a fish out of water. She was breathing with great difficulty. I cannot describe her suffering. Her beautiful face became very ugly with lots of burnt marks and she was looking terrible. She was dying. My father cannot sleep without sleeping pills. He also woke up after listening her screaming and came there. He started shouting at my brother –

"What have you done idiot? You are a panchayet election candidate. You will go to jail for lifetime if your crime is proved. You must control your anger. You are behaving like a wild animal."

He was standing like a stone devoid of feelings with angry red eyes.

"Papa please stop lecturing. Take her to hospital immediately or else she will die." - I said to my father.

"Hospital!!! Don't make this mistake. If she remains alive and gives her statement to police, we all will spend rest of our life in jail. She must have to die otherwise we will die."

"No papa. Please save her."

I was helpless and so was my mom and younger sister. My

father locked us in our room and strictly ordered to keep quiet and threatened not to say anything to anyone. We did not dare to say anything to anyone. My younger sister lost her consciousness after watching the terribly burnt body and face of Fatima. Loud Hindi music sound was coming as a function of music and dance was going on there in the panchayat meeting place of the village. The local village club had arranged this as they do every year. The whole villagers went there to enjoy the night. My father hit upon a plan. My father and brother opened the gas of cylinder and threw fire and it burst very soon with loud noise. The sound was so loud that the villagers who were deep drowned in the ocean of music and dance woke up. Many people rushed to our home. The kitchen was badly damaged. People discovered different parts of Fatima's body from here and there. Women were heard crying. Men were shouting a lot. Police came and did the investigation. It was recorded as an accident. Fatima's body pieces were sent for postmortem. Her parents were informed about the incidents and they rushed from their village to our house. No one was able to stop her father who was crying like a child and so was her mother. Later her elder sister arrived. We were so deeply shocked that we were neither crying nor speaking. We became stone. My father and elder brother were crying and acting wisely as if they have lost a precious thing. They did play their role well. Nothing happened to my father and elder brother. It was an accident. My brother won lot of sympathy from villagers as he lost his wife in a terrible gas tragedy and won the election. He got a handsome amount from the insurance company as he insured her life. People used to talk about the incident many days and after months they forgot all about it. We also forgot all about it. After that gradually we all started living a normal life forgetting the past. But it put a permanent scratch in my heart. Whenever I remember that incident and her terrible ugly burnt face I lose my normalcy. But what can I do in this jungle? I also started adjusting to live a happy life like a selfish person. Now I don't feel that much. What is the value of the feelings? Most probably nothing! My younger sister was given treatment for a long time under a psychiatrist. Later she was admitted in boarding school to erase everything from her mind. Now she is staying in hostel. Now I don't mind this so deeply."

"So sad! Poor Fatima! May Allah bless her and grant her Jannah (Heaven). Sure Allah will do justice with her. She will get justice from Allah."

"Allah! Justice! Justice??? What a nice joke! The same thing Fatima's father said again and again and consoled himself. Really it's a nice joke."

"No Sana – it is not a joke. Allah is swift in his account of justice and surely he will do justice. Wait and see - he will punish your brother."

"Really Allah will punish my brother??? I don't think so. See the irony of life - my brother is enjoying his luxury life. He is going to marry an extremely beautiful and smart girl. He is in love with her. She is from a wealthy Hindu family. He has purchased a new luxury house in the town and a luxury car. Last Sunday we visited his new house – full of luxurious amenities. I don't know whether Fatima will be granted a Jannah but my brother is going to live in Heaven very soon in his luxurious house."

"Don't speak like a kaafer! (non-believer). This is temporary pleasure. We must not forget that this life is very short. Our real everlasting life is awaiting after death. Each soul will get its reward according to its deed in this life. We are here only to give a test and indeed it is a very short life. According to our deeds in this life we will either enjoy luxury life in Heaven eternally or will be burnt in fire forever in Hell."

"Fatima used to pray five times daily, every year she observed 30 days fasting during Ramzan, she used to love people – poor and rich equally, she gave respect to the servants. She was so pious and devout to Allah. But I saw her to get burnt alive in hell here. I don't know whether she will live in peace in Jannah or not but she is burnt in hell fire alive and I have seen it with my own eyes. Where was Allah when she was screaming that night? Why did He not save her? Where was His mercy? How did He allow her devout pious lady to get burnt alive? I don't know what was her crime for which she had to pay her life in a horrible death."

"Sana, have patience and you see one day she will get justice. I am sure."

"Let's see if she gets justice."

We remained silent for a moment.

"My father is a Muslim – only for name sake as I have never seen him to pray or to go to mosque – not even on Fridays or to observe fasting for Allah. He never cares for the basic fundamentals of Islam. He is living a lofty proudly life. And so are my brothers and in fact me also. Me and my mother try to observe fasting during Ramazan but quits after 4 or 5 fastings. Still you see – my father and brothers are living in AC home, moving here and there in AC car. They have power, position and authority. People of the village respect them. They have earned huge money to live a luxurious life. What else they need to live?"

"It is very sad but true part of our society. Leave the topic. You will be getting late for marriage party."

"Yeah. Now I don't care for such things. I forget to feel now. Whenever and wherever getting chance I am enjoying my life. What will happen tomorrow we don't know? So it is better to enjoy the present forgetting the past. That I am doing."

"Good. It is a very nice approach to enjoy life. Can you please bring that assignment paper? We will find the answers."

"Yes, I will do that. I don't why I told you all these things. I did not hesitate to tell you a grave secret of my family. May be my heart has full trust in you. You have become very close to me."

"I also trust you Sana. I also feel you are very close to my heart. We share many things without hesitation."

"Really you feel me very close to your heart."

"Yes. I do."

Sana brought the assignment paper and gave it to me.

"I will bring some cold drink."

She went to bring some cold drink. As I was searching for content to find answer of the questions given in the assignment from the internet, an adult site opens up containing exclusive adult material. It excited me. Though I closed the tab quickly but I was very much interested to see it. Sana came with cold drink and we enjoyed it as she took another chair and sat beside me. Now she seemed to be happy and cheerful. She started making some fun also.

"I did not see your father and brothers at home today. Are they not at home?"

"Aslam and Papa are gone to Delhi for five days. They

have some business meetings. Asraaf (elder brother) hardly stays at home. He is staying at his new home in the town. He is very busy with his party."

"How is your sister?"

"She is fine. She is doing her higher secondary from a boarding school. She is staying in hostel."

The weather was changing. It seemed that it was going to rain very soon. Very soon dark cloud covered the sky and it started raining heavily. An aunty (lady servant) came and kept a bottle of cool water and took cold drink glasses. Sana asked her

"How is mom now?"

"She is fine. She is sleeping."

"Ok." The aunty left the room.

"As I was searching a topic in google, that adult site appeared again. Actually it was not closed – it remained minimized without my knowledge. I was confused. I was trying to close it quickly.

"Very hot site yaar! Wait! Wait!"

I was totally silent. I was confused. I was at a loss. Sana went to the door and closed it. She came and sat on my thigh.

"Can you love me?"

"Yes I love you."

"Then please love me…"

She hugs me affectionately and start kissing me. I was afraid if I got caught red handed I would be killed by her brothers. Soon she submitted her virgin to me. I also lost control. We had our first sex. She was very curious and so was I.

After this also she used to call me at her home whenever she was alone. We used to enjoy. How did this lovely and sexy girl refuse sex to her husband? I was in confusion. My heart was not ready to believe the incident happened to Sana as narrated by Juber to me. How did this happen? But I feel very sad for her.

Chapter - III

My mother entered my room and saw my sad face.

"What happened? You are looking so sad! What is the wrong with you?"

"No mom, nothing is wrong – I am fine."

"But you do not look fine. Tell me is there any problem. If you share your problem with me, your mental burden will decrease. I may find some good solution also. Please tell me what the problem is."

"I don't have any problem mom. Have you heard anything about Sana?"

"Yes she went to her in-law's house yesterday after her marriage. The whole villagers know this. She is married to a very rich man. She will lead a happy and luxurious life there. Are you still missing her? You are feeling sad as she is married to someone. Dear son make sensible demand in life according to your family status. You know very well that we tried but her father was too proud to talk to us."

"I am not feeling sad for that mom. Today morning she is admitted in hospital."

"Hospital! But why is she admitted in hospital? Is there any big problem?"

"She is brutally beaten and raped by her husband."

"Raped by her husband! I have never heard such thing that a woman can be raped by her husband. It is unbelievable!! After all he is her husband. We cannot say it rape."

"But it has happened with her mom."

"I know that still you love her. But don't think any nonsense thing like raped by husband. How can a wife be raped by her husband? People will laugh."

"Today morning she is admitted in hospital as she received serious injury. Her family went to rescue her. Juber also went with Aslam and he told me the incident - whatever he saw there."

"Really she is injured seriously!"

"Her husband has beaten her brutally like an animal. She is not able to breathe properly. She is groaning in pain."

"Just you think why a newly married wife will be beaten badly on first night by her husband. There is something wrong either in the wife or in the groom."

"Her husband is an animal. Nothing can be wrong from Sana's side as I know her well."

"We cannot say this so easily. She is an open girl and maintains relationship with multiple boys. May be her husband has seen her secret messages or caught her talking over phone with her ex-boyfriends. We have heard a lot of such things about her recently. She never wears hijab or remains under control as a girl. She does not look like a Muslim girl from any point of view. Her full family is like that. They are blind with their wealth. Thank God that her father rejected your marriage proposal with her."

"Mom please don't think so. If a girl mixes with boys freely, it does not mean that she has lost her character. She is a nice girl. I know her."

"Her father is an over proud man. He didn't talk to your father properly when your father went to him for your marriage proposal with Sana. Rather he insulted your father."

"Mom please forget the past. Don't live in past. It is a very bad habit. Think about the present and try to live in present. Don't get lost in past and don't be anxious of future."

"Alhamdulillah! I am very happy with my present. I am very much thankful to Allah and to your father. By the grace of Allah, you father has given us a very happy and peaceful life though we are not having a luxurious life like Mr Jafar (Sana's father). I don't live in past. I think nowadays you are living in past more and you have ignored the present totally. You are wasting time in searching better job and writing competitive exams. For last four years you are working hard to prepare yourself for civil service exam, bank po exam and other government job exam. You have tried your best. Success is not for all. May be Allah has something much better for you. Now you are in search of private job that has no future. I think you are burning midnight lamp in preparing competitive exams and interviews and you are ignoring your present for better but uncertain future. We don't know what will happen tomorrow − even about very next moment but we are planning a lot for a great future. Why don't you start working in our farm with your father? Marry someone according to your level and live a happy peaceful life. We will search a good girl for you. We don't want luxurious life − we want peaceful life. Your father's earning is limited still we are living happily and enjoying our present."

"Ok mom, please stop your lecture. Enjoying present! What are enjoying mom? We don't have a good house. We don't have enough cash to meet all demands. We don't have quality amenities in the house to live a happy life. How can you enjoy a happy and peaceful life? My friends are having nice bikes, branded dress and costly mobiles. But I don't have any of them. I feel very ashamed when I see them with these things."

"My dear son, lifeless branded materials can never bring peace in life. They only excite our desire making our life a hell. You will never get peace unless You abandon material desire and please don't compare and compete with others. This is the main reason of woe and misery in the world today. None is satisfied in this world with what he has as he has grown the habit of comparing and competing with others. If you waste your time in comparing and competing with others, you will have no time to enjoy what you have in your hand. That's why Allah has forbidden mankind to compare and compete with each other. It is a dangerous disease of our society and spreading like cancer."

"But the whole world is in competition. All are running race madly!"

"See my son people have learnt to build very beautiful and attractive houses with lots of amenities but the people who are living there are having very ugly hearts – they cannot make that house a home. If there is no homely touch in the house then what is the use of the large beautiful house. You can see Mr. Jafar's house as the live example of this. Be content with what Allah has given you. People are wearing fashionable dresses to look beautiful and attractive but they have lost inner beauty – the beauty of heart. Most probably to hide the inner ugliness people are wearing more and more costly dresses."

"Ok mom. Please stop preaching. I have understood."

"Your father was feeling sad as you are not going to mosque for five regular compulsory prayers. He was saying you are not in touch with Quran and Sunnah of our Prophet Muhamed (pbuh). He is anxious about your present and future. See my son Allah has not guaranteed old age to all – our death is certain and it can come anytime anywhere. So be prepared. Each soul has to taste death – men-women, black-white, rich-poor, young-old and they will return to their permanent home - to their Lord. Each soul will get its reward according to its deeds."

"Mom please stop preaching me these old things. I know these things very well."

"I know you are feeling bored with my words. But this is the truth. Listen to me you better start working in our farm with your father. Here you can live a life full of peace. It is better to live a life in peace than living a life in prosperity and luxury devoid of peace. Day before yesterday your friend Jayanta came with his wife to meet us. They have purchased a big house in the city. Both husband and wife are doing job. They are earning well. They have bought a new car also. But when I asked them how their life in the city is, they gave a very grave reply – "We are leading a life of a machine." They told that they don't have time for each other. They are having very busy schedule. On weekends also they are getting engaged in different works. That Jayanta who was unhappy with his old home is still sad in his new house. He was saying that morning he is going to office regularly and evening he is coming back and only the night he is passing in his house with burdens of office works. Earlier he was not having money to eat good food and to live in luxurious house. But now he has money and luxurious house but no time to eat and live there. He told that he has become a slave of his daily routine. So is the fate of his wife. She is also so busy with her job that she has no time and passion to make that house a home. His parents went to live with him but came back to their village home within a month as they cannot find men and women made of blood and flesh with feelings living in the house. They are busy in saving money and paying EMI of their home loan and car loan. They are leading a restless life. No time to think or thank or remember God. Whatever free time they have is consumed to plan their future. How bad luck the baby is who is born in their house! The baby is loved and cared by an ayah. They don't have time to love their own baby. May Allah lead us to the right path."

"Mom I know it is the fact. It is a common story of our modern life. But we cannot help it. We need money to get born, to live and to die. Without money we cannot imagine anything. If you have money you have everything."

"May Allah guide you to the right path. You are fully entrapped in the net of Satan. May Allah save you from the whispering of Satan – the eternal enemy of Mankind. If fact the people of the whole world are entrapped in the net of Satan. They don't have time to remember and thank Allah, their creator. So how will they get inner satisfaction or a content life. The more they will earn the less they will be satisfied. That's why all people are busy in comparing and competing with each other. What they think as development and prosperity but actually this very development and prosperity will ruin them forever."

I understood that my mom was not in a mood to stop her preaching and I was really feeling very bored. So I left my room saying that I am going to meet one of my friends. I understood without job or good earning it was quite difficult to live in the society like a man. Whatever my mom has said is the true fact but I have a big dream to become a rich man. After completing graduation I felt the extreme need of a job. Some of my friends managed to get jobs either in private or in government sector. But only a few friends were lucky to get job. Many of my friends are having same fate like me. We are madly searching for a job – in fact any job. To get a job I am madly attending multiple interviews in different cities and writing competitive examinations for government job and taking coaching classes to prepare myself for those competitive examinations. In the beginning I started searching for a job with extra confidence and less care and I have attended quite a number of interviews. But till now I cannot find any progress in getting a job. Now I really feel tired sometime. My parents told me to do farming. My father has enough land in our village to feed us. But who cares for feeding. I was growing my dreams day by day in the field of my life.

My phone rings. I looked at the screen of my phone and it was a call from an unknown number. I received the call -

"Hello. Am I talking to Mr Sohail?"

"Yes speaking."

"Sir this is Shruti from Sigma Job Consultancy. We have received your resume as you are searching for a job."

"Yes madam I am searching for a job."

"You are shortlisted. You have to attend interview tomorrow in Delhi. Details of the venue of interview we will email and sms you."

"Yes madam please sms me the address."

"So should I confirm that you are coming to attend the interview?"

"Yes madam you can confirm. I will come to attend the

interview."

"But for confirmation you have to pay Rs 500 registration fees now using internet banking or debit card. I have sent a link to your email for the payment. Once your payment is completed a slip will be generated in the system. You have to take a print copy of the same and you have to bring it to attend the interview. Please complete your payment as soon as possible because vacancies are limited."

"Ok madam. I will do that by evening. I will go to internet café and complete the payment."

"Ok bye bye... Wish you all the best in getting your dream job with Sigma Job Consultancy."

"Ok madam. Thank you very much."

I came home immediately as it was 4pm. I went to my mom.

"Mom I need some money."

"What will you do with money?"

"Tonight I am starting for Delhi. Tomorrow I have an interview. I am short-listed to attend an interview for a job."

"But all of a sudden ……"

"It does not matter mom. I will make over night train journey and tomorrow I will reach there early in the morning."

"Do you have confirmed ticket?"

"How will I have confirmed ticket? Now only I am informed about the interview."

"But without confirmed ticket it is very difficult to make overnight train journey. You won't get berth to sleep."

"Don't worry mom. I will manage a seat with the help of TTE."

"Ok I will ask for money from you father. He is gone to

mosque to offer afternoon prayer now. Let him come home."

"Ok I am going to the internet café to make an online payment and to take a print copy of the payment receipt. You please take money from father and keep with you."

"Rs 500 will be enough or you need more."

"If possible manage Rs 1000 as I have to purchase some competition exam preparation magazines and books in Delhi."

"Ok. I will try."

I started going towards the internet café situated in the town 4 km away from my village. When I reached there I was surprised to see it was fully crowded. Actually tomorrow there is a competitive exam for Group-D in Delhi. Many candidates are taking print out of their exam admit card. Many boys are playing video games in the café – in fact they are playing very dangerous game full of violence. No system was free. He told me to wait for one hour. I went to another café but the situation was same there also. Anyway I had to wait for my turn. I made the payment and took the print out and started for home. I got an sms. It was a message from the bank about the debit of Rs 500 from my account and it showed Rs 357.65 was the balance left in my account. Another message I got. It was from Sigma Job Consultancy. I got the address of my interview venue in Delhi. I hurried towards home because I have to get ready and come back here again to catch a train at night. Daily 3 or 4 trains pass during night through this route and they have stoppage at this station. I came back home. As I entered home I got a nice smell of food being cooked for dinner. I went straight to mom in the kitchen. She was busy in making some special food.

"Mom have you taken money from father?"

"Yes your father has given Rs 500 as he is not having more at the moment. I will give Rs 300 that I have saved for last three months."

"I think this much is enough. Thank you very much."

"Say thanks to Allah. We cannot give anything to anyone without His grace. When Allah will give you it will be more than your expectation."

"Ok mom I will get ready soon."

"You get ready. I have prepared dinner early for you."

"Thank you very much mom."

My sisters come and ask

"Brother you are going to Delhi. Can you please bring some colourful glass bangles from Delhi for us?"

"Who will give money?" I asked with a smile.

"We will give you money."

"Ok then I will bring if I get time."

They gave me Rs 80 for bringing glass bangles. Meantime my father calls me. I went to him –

"Yes Papa. Did you call me?"

"At least say salaam to me. It will give you inner strength."

"Sorry Papa. Asalamo alikum Papa."

"Walekum Asalam."

There was a pause for a moment. After few seconds my father asks -

"Which interview are you going to attend tomorrow?"

"It is organized by a Job consultancy. Many companies will participate and directly recruit candidates."

"For which post you are short-listed?"

"For sales executive."

"So you want to become a sales executive. You will be selling the assigned products door to door. You are ready to become a salesman. But you have problem to work in your own farm just because you don't like farming and it will degrade your prestige among friends."

"Not only this Papa, there is no future in farming. Farmers are committing suicide. Everyday news is showing what a terrible life these farmers are leading. There is no chance to earn more. There is no way for getting promotion. My life will become stagnant. All progress of my life will stop if I take farming as my profession. Even I cannot manage my own expenses from farming. I cannot live like you."

"Ok. After all it is your life. You have to decide what is best for you. May Allah fulfill your wish and lead you on the right path of honesty."

For a moment we remained silent.

"So how much salary will they offer?"

"Let me get first selected – now only shortlisted. Salary will be decided based on my performance in interview."

"Have you booked ticket?"

"No. I will manage it with the TTE."

"Try to manage a ticket. Otherwise it will be very difficult to do night journey."

"Yes. I will try."

"Ok. May Allah bless you."

My elder sister called me for dinner. I had finished my dinner quickly. Mom made delicious chicken biriyani but my mind was so busy that hardly I can enjoy its taste. After finishing dinner I got ready for the station.

"Have you taken all necessary documents for interview?" – asks mom.

"Yes I have taken."

"Please check once again else you will be in problem there if you forget any."

"Yes mom I have checked it well. I have taken all necessary documents."

I took my bicycle and started moving towards the station. My mind became busy and many past interactions with my father got flashed in my mind as I was riding my bicycle alone on the moon-lit road.

My father is very much happy with his agriculture and sweet home and lovely village and his beloved family that was his heart. But I don't like cultivation. It will be my prestige issue if I work in the field of my father as a farmer – especially after passing graduation. I need a good earning job for a better life-style – an apple i-phone in hand, a stylish bike or if possible a car, branded pants, shirts, shoes, costly TV with big screen, fashioned home, pets, multiple girlfriends and of course a modern beautiful smart wife and enough cash to fulfill her demands. My father doesn't have big ambition in his life. His demands in life are limited. In fact he is leading a happy and content life in his village. He goes to the nearby town for marketing when he needs seeds, manure or any household items. He is always busy with his farming work and more busy in the remembrance of Allah. He regularly offers five compulsory prayers and observes one month fasting (Ramzan) every year and works hard to keep his family happy. He is always content with what he has – hardly has he made any complain for not having this or that. He always gives thanks to Allah by saying 'Alhamdulillah' for every small things or happiness. Sometimes he wakes up at mid-night and starts special prayer (Tahajjud) in the remembrance of Almighty Allah and sometimes he starts crying like a child asking for His forgiveness or praying for others – for the peace of the world. He disturbs our sleep early in the morning as he calls us for morning first prayer (Fazar). My mother and sisters will get up early in the morning for prayer except me. I used to watch TV late night and naturally I had to sleep more in late morning. My father loves me a lot but sometimes he shouts at me as I have developed some bad habits with my friends. I don't pray regularly nor do I observe fasting during the holy month of Ramzan. In my family all listen to my father's order and follows his instructions strictly not being afraid but for the sake of his love and care. His family is his whole world – hardly has he done anything for self, whatever he is doing only to bring happiness and prosperity in the family. He remains happy with small things. He himself cooks special food on every Friday for all of us – and really the food he cooks on Friday is extremely delicious and the whole family enjoys it. He regularly helps mom in daily household works and I have never noticed him to be angry at my mom or sisters. But sometimes he becomes angry at me – he exerts his anger of love and care when I do something that he doesn't like. Sometimes he will take a long counseling class of mine quoting from the noble Quran and Prophet Muhamed's (pbuh) life. He was anxious of my worldly life as well as the life after this world. He always tries to teach us to follow the right path. I sometimes express sadness as we don't have a big house, good sources of income, motorcycle, big screen TV, good bank balance etc like my other friends. My father will say to me with his soothing words to make me happy – "Express your gratitude to Almighty Allah that you have regular meals, a roof to take shelter, a happy family to take care of you, good health. Many people don't have this much also. Many people are suffering a lot in this world. So be grateful to Allah for having these things. Try to enjoy what you have, don't feel sad for those things that you are not having." And he advises me not to compare and compete with others in terms of wealth, health, beauty, power or position. He continues to say that these things are temporary – these things will lead us to temptation, the great sin – Satan diverts us with these ugly things - these things may be today in someone's hand and tomorrow it may go to other's hand. But your character and Imaan (honesty) will remain with you forever here in this world and you will find a great reward after this world. Why people cry for those ugly and temporary things (beauty, power or position, wealth etc) – we cannot carry them with us after our death which is sure to come any time. Nothing is real in this world except death – nothing is sure in this world except death. You must have to return to Him from Whom you came here. Here you came to give your test and after that you will get reward according to your work – perpetual peaceful happy luxurious life in Heaven if you do good deeds or everlasting unbearable torture and pain in the fire of Hell for wrong doers. If you have lead an honest and just life – you will enjoy this worldly life and of course the life after death in heaven which is permanent. So don't compare and compete with others. If you do so, you will forget to enjoy whatever you have in your hand. Rather be thankful to Allah who has given you nice eyes to see, ears to hear, mouth to eat and speak, tongue to taste and legs to go or hands to do good work. There are many people in this world who don't have all these things – they don't have two regular meals or a roof to get shelter. They suffer a lot – you must be happy and thankful to Allah who has given you so many things. After listening my father's lectures, I used to feel bored and sometimes uneasy. But when I sit alone or sit with a sad heart, my father's words echoes in my ears and seem to be very true. But again I forget and become busy with my friends to enjoy my life. As I rode on my bicycle thinking all these, I reached station very soon. I kept my bicycle in the cycle stand by paying Rs 5 and went to the ticket counter to get a ticket. But the counter was full of people. I was waiting in a long queue to get ticket. Only one ticket counters was in operation out of three ticket counters. I heard an announcement that a train is coming soon on platform no 2 bound to Delhi. Actually this train was scheduled to pass at 4 pm but it was running six hours late. I had least chance to catch this train as I need to stand in queue at least 30 minutes to get my ticket. Many people standing in queue like me started shouting at the counter man – "Brother please hurry up. Give ticket fast. Train is coming soon. Fast! Fast!"

But it did not reach to him. He was issuing tickets using the computer in a slow pace searching each letter and numbers one by one from the keyboard through his big and powerful eye glasses.

The train reached on the platform. Many people ran towards the train without taking ticket fearing that they may lose the train as it will stop here only for 2 or 3 minutes. If they wait for ticket they may lose it. So I also went to catch this train without ticket. But it was over crowded. I talked to the TTE if he can manage a berth but he replied that there is no berth in sleeper or ac coach. I cannot dare to travel in general coaches as there was no space to put my feet. So I came back again to the ticket counter but this time the queue was longer than before. Already I made enough progress in the queue earlier but now again I had to start from the last. Anyhow after waiting and standing in the long queue for a long time I managed to get the ticket.

Chapter - IV

I was waiting for the next train in the station. It seemed that the station was more over crowded compare to other days. A man came and requested to mange little space for him so that he can also sit on the platform seat where I was already sitting. Unwillingly I managed little space for him. As he sat down, I lost the comfort of sitting. After sitting he started reading an evening newspaper.

"Why this much crowd? It is not even festive season." He asked me casually.

"Tomorrow there is a Group-D exam for government job. I think that is the main reason of this crowd."

"There is an open rally for recruitment in army in Agra cant tomorrow. For that also crowd is too much." - said another man who was sitting beside me.

"Day by day the number of unemployed youths is increasing at a fast speed. If they get any vacancy information they will rush there in large number." - said another man.

"Last week Public Service Commission has received five lakhs seventy thousand eight hundred and forty six applications for 52 clerk posts. Now can you imagine how many unemployed persons are there in the society." – said the man who was reading newspaper.

"Government is sleeping. It does not take step to generate employment. It is totally careless for the welfare of the unemployed youth."

"How much government will do alone? People are also responsible for this."

"How people are responsible? What people will do if there is no place to work?"

"Actually tendency is changing. All want only government job. We don't want to send our children to government school, we don't like to get treatment from government hospitals – but we all want government job."

"Government should privatize these sectors. Many people will get job and public will also get good service."

"How public will get good service? Our political leaders are corrupted. They are hoarding the mountains of money. They don't care for public."

"Actually many people are working in private sectors but they cannot find job security like government sector and work load is too high. That's why all want only government job. If government properly supervise and control working condition and salary and security of job in private sector, people can work peacefully there."

"We are living in a dangerous age. See the news headlines; you can understand what an uncertain life we are leading. Local, national and international news everywhere horrible news are there – rape, murder, riot, bombing, air striking, dangerous virus attack, terrorist attack, scams, corruption, burning alive, cheating and looting….."

An announcement is heard. According to this announcement the train we are waiting for is delayed by 2 hours.

An old man was also sitting with us. He started saying a long unending theory.

"Human being is destroying itself. Now the trend is changed. We are trying to be modern – even ultra modern. But actually this is leading us to be primitive. Now youth has lost total interest in agriculture. And government is also totally ignorant. Farmers are committing suicide. Government is trying to increase industrialization and encouraging corporate and service sector. Government's effort to boost agriculture is almost nothing. Human can survive in this earth without industrialization and corporate sector but human existence cannot be possible without agriculture. Agriculture has vast potentiality. We are eating bad quality food mixed with artificial things or grown using chemical fertilizer. Due to modernization and industrialization we have made so much progress that plastic rice is available in market – we will soon start eating plastic. As a result dangerous diseases are becoming common and human growth and strength is decreasing. Days are not so far when human strength and thinking power will get transferred to machine – we all know about robots and artificial intelligence. We made money as servant but now it has become a most powerful master. Same way these machines will become our master one day. Living will become impossible without them….."

I was getting bored. It was very difficult to pass time. Anyway after 2 and half hours the train arrived. We all became busy in getting a seat but this train was also full. I tried to get into the general compartment but it was so full that it was impossible to get inside. Even I cannot put my feet on the pedal as people were hanging from the door. I mentally got prepared to make a horrible train journey. Yes it was really a horrible journey! People were doing journey like animals – better to say like some things packed as much as possible. But things are packed with care so that they do not get damaged but in this general compartment people were packed in a worst condition. I was wondering how they will breathe. So I tried to get a place in the sleeper coach. Believe me the sleeper compartment had no place to put my two legs properly. You cannot imagine how a compartment which has capacity of seventy two persons was carrying more than two hundred people – men and women. It was the situation of a sleeper class compartment. People were hanging from the door. The journey was not for one or two hours – at least six hours. Now imagine what a horrible journey it was – standing in a fully crowded compartment whole night without sleeping. Problem will increase when someone needs to alight – going for toilet from the middle of the compartment. He or she has to struggle hard to get a path to the toilet room. In case of emergency what will happen God knows. Still people make fun, laugh, talk and the expert tea sellers or other vendors will entertain the passengers with their calls – "Tea, tea, tea, coffee, coffee, coffee, cigarette, bidi, gutkha, pan masala. boiled eggs etc. These vendors are expert – they will manage a path inside the fully crowded compartment and they will sell also. Really it is a great art! What a big expert they are! They can manage a path but I cannot because I am not an expert like them. But I have to make journey in this train anyhow. Otherwise I won't be able to reach Delhi to attend the interview. I saw a TTE. I approached to him to arrange a seat in sleeper coach but he was surrounded by many people who had same fate like me. All are trying to allure him with money to get a seat. But he refused saying that there are no vacant berths. I had previous experiences of such horrible train journey. It is not that other day the train is not crowded. But today it is extremely crowded. Sleeper class passengers who have paid good fare for a berth are also facing unwanted trouble and not able to do a comfortable journey. In spite of this worse situation people are talking, laughing, shouting, joking. It was midnight. The train is moving at a limited speed as the dense fog was there. Outside it is very cold and one can feel the silence that prevails outside except the train's noise. Nothing can be seen as the fog was thick. After two hours journey I was not able to stand properly and there was no place to sit. The train stopped at a station. I started searching for a TTE again expecting that if any berth is vacated as some passengers got down there. I met a TTE and asked to manage a seat. He told that he can offer a seat in AC if I can pay him Rs 1000. But I didn't have that much money with me. I requested him very politely and gently and he agreed with Rs 500. Finally I got a berth in AC. Here it was not overcrowded and inside it was rather comfortable. Almost all the passengers are sleeping. I also tried to sleep. But the TTE told me that someone will come to claim the seat in the next station and I have to vacate it. He will manage another seat as someone will get down also. I agreed and tried to sleep. Three hours are over but no one came to claim that seat as the train was late. Due to fog and railway technical problem, the train was not getting green signal. It was halting here and there for hours and moving slowly. Now it was morning and nobody came to claim that seat. I saw the passengers are getting up from their sleep. The midnight noise of that coach was still ringing in my ears – especially jokes and laughing and vendor's sale shouting. But the AC coach is almost silence. Passengers sitting here are busy within themselves as if they have forgotten to talk and laugh openly and heartily. All seems to carry tons of tension. Anyway I reached Delhi three hours late. I caught a bus bound to my destination and reached the hotel where interview was going on. I had got refreshed in the train itself and had tea and biscuit at the station. The registration counter was also surrounded by many persons like me. Someone came and told the candidates to make a queue for registration smoothly. We all followed that obediently. I was waiting as my number was 79 and my turn will come after 78 candidates. As I was sitting and waiting, many past events flashed in my mind and I became reminiscent for a moment remembering old days in school and college. How happy and care free were those days – all demands were fulfilled by our parents. After waiting upto 2 pm, I was not able to control my hunger as my stomach was deliberately demanding some food. I enquired at the registration counter when my turn will come, the counter girl in her beautiful attire and sweet voice told me to wait for a couple of hours more. A couple of hours more! I went outside to have some food. I found a street vendor selling hot and spicy food 'chhole batture' for Rs 20 per plate and without thinking anything I galloped one plate. I can never find the nice taste of food sold on street in AC hotels – I always enjoy the street food as it does not cut my pocket that much. I had a bad habit of smoking cigarette and I was longing for one. But I was in suspicion of the smell as it may disturb the interviewer. But I can manage the smell by chewing some mouth fresheners. So I enjoyed smoking a cigarette and started chewing mouth freshener. I went back to the hotel where interview was in progress. I sat on a chair and was waiting for my turn. Now candidate no 42 is going for interview. 2 hours over – time was around 5 pm. After half an hour someone came and informed to the rest of the waiting candidates that the interview is postponed for tomorrow. We have to come tomorrow. They will follow the same order. So we all started to move and find some shelter in the city to pass the night as outside it was very cold. But it was quite difficult to find a shelter as the cost of room rent was too high. I had spent my money to get a seat in the train. Now I have around Rs 400 only. I was searching for a Dharmashala for a cheaper accommodation but all were filled. It was late evening. I heard Azan (night prayer call) from a mosque. I was not used to pray regularly except Friday special Prayer. So I didn't pay heed to this. I found a street vendor selling chicken biriyani for Rs 50 full plate and Rs 30 half plate. I filled my stomach with a plate of chicken biriyani. It was hot, spicy and very tasty. I started searching for a cheap shelter here and there. I saw a big building and many people were making their bed at the front open space under the hanging roof of the building – most of them were beggars and labourers. They have no home in the city but they manage to live like that. It was already 9 pm. I was totally exhausted and had no plan to search any more as my legs were not ready to co-operate. So I also tried to manage a space there. I arranged my bed by unfolding some newspapers and put my bag to be used as pillow. But it was very cold and the floor was cold too. It seemed very difficult to sleep. I took out my shawl from the bag and wrapped myself. I saw many of them were drinking some cheap local liquor to escape the cold and to get rid of the pain due to the day's labour. I was looking at them. One of them offered me a glass of liquor – I didn't deny the offer.

Sometimes I used to drink with my friends occasionally and secretly. I had friends from multiple religions and caste and I had full faith that they will never inform this to my father. My father is a strict person and he practices Islam as much as possible – money doesn't matter to him but dignity matters. They were eating something and were talking with each other – nothing serious or important – it was all about their daily life. They were eating, talking, joking, laughing and drinking. They were homeless but you cannot trace any disappointment in their face for not having a home. They have nothing still they were happy. It was very cold but they did not complain for it. As I was a new comer in the folk, I was not able to mingle with them instantly but I also contributed little joke and had a laugh with them. It made me forget the ordeal day. I was thinking many things but actually nothing. I can hear the snoring noise from some of them. They all are sleeping a sound sleep under their old, dirty and torn blanket. Vehicles were moving at a moderate speed but number of vehicles decreased and nobody can be seen on the street. It was completely silent. The road was getting covered with fog and gradually the tall buildings got covered with dense fog. Street lights became dim due to the dense fog. Now the road also started taking rest and seemed that it was going to sleep as the nature is going to wrap it with her foggy blanket and very few vehicles were passing. The weary city road was sleeping, people were sleeping – in fact the whole city was sleeping. Deep darkness covered the city as the King of Darkness, Satan, is going to reign. Nature covered the city in darkness to hide it from the evil eye of Satan – to save it from the danger of Satan. Only I was not able to sleep as I was not accustomed to it. I can hear the sound of the patrolling police van. I also hear the sound of an ambulance. Later a fire extinguisher vehicle was moving at a high speed making its special sound. The city became completely silent. Hours before how the streets were crowded with people of different attire and fashion and made it more live when the band of beautiful girls was passing in the evening with their friends in modern attire. The road was restless with unnumbered vehicles and traffic here and there. Now it is completely silent. All are sleeping.

People prefer to live in this concrete jungle. We all like to have a home in the city – the jungle of concrete – without a heart or feeling. We all know cities are heartless - still we like it. If someone comes in my village at night like me, he / she will never have to pass the night under open sky or on the street because someone will offer food and shelter – it's sure. My village people may not be as rich as this city people but they are much richer by heart. They have small house but still they will arrange a shelter for a person in need. My village is very nice and beautiful. But it cannot give me a job of my choice. So I leave it and come to city in search of job. Again my mind started to get the flashes of my past. If I was at home my mother will force me to drink a glass of hot milk sometimes with turmeric powder which I dislike. But I miss it a lot in this severe cold. My soft and comfortable bed will be cleaned and ready either by mom or by my sisters. I am the prince of my home. Uh! It is too cold to bear – the floor, the wind – all cold. How they are sleeping!

Chapter - V

It was midnight. Suddenly I heard a sharp scream – a deep scream of heavy pain and torture. When I heard this I was little drowsy due to that liquor and others were sleeping – in fact the whole city was sleeping as if all have drunk the liquor of carelessness, heartlessness and ignorance. The sharp scream became sharper and it was coming from an oncoming bus and the scream was unbearable and it pierced my heart when the bus came very close to me and passed. The scream got fade as the bus moved away from me. It was not heard anymore when the bus went out of my sight. I tried to awake myself to help the victim. But I was too tired to walk and my legs became senseless and frozen due to the severing cold. I found that my legs were not under my control. I tried to get control over them and soon blood started flowing to the veins of my legs and they started becoming active again. It was the screaming sound of a girl who has become a prey of some animals in the jungle of concrete. I cannot ignore this. I tried to stand straight but still I felt my legs were not fully active. I kept trying and soon my legs become active. But it was too late. I sat back. I thought to inform police the matter by dialing 100. So I took my mobile from the bag but unfortunately it was dead as the battery was over. "What will happen to that girl! Oh Allah save her." I started praying for her as I learnt this from my father. My father taught us prayer has great strength, it can do impossible things possible – possible and impossible concept is in our mind only and there is nothing impossible for Allah, the great and the Creator of the universe. So I also started praying for her. But will Allah accept my prayer because I am not as devout to Allah as my father and I hardly follow the practical rules of Islam taught by my father. I don't pray five times, I don't complete all 30 fastings in the sacred month of Ramzan – after 2 or 3 I skipped showing lame excuse. If my father starts shouting at me, my mother will become a safeguard. My father taught me Zina (unlawful sexual relation or adultery) is a great crime in Islam whether you do it openly, forcibly or secretly – you have to pay for it in this world and after this world – ocean of fire will be waiting for the criminal to burn him or her eternally. So don't commit adultery sin but I did. I was trapped in the net of love of a girl and ignored study and became busy to satisfy her thirst secretly. Though I also got pleasure but it was a temporary pleasure. It didn't last long. She left me as I was no more useful because her marriage was arranged with a rich person by her parents and she easily forgot me. She used me as her time pass toy and an object of enjoyment. My father occasionally used to teach all of us the basic things of Islam – not to hurt anyone, not to laugh at anyone, not to usurp anyone's money or property, not to tell lie, not to kill any human (if you kill a human it will be assumed that you have killed the whole humanity), not to commit adultery sin, not to have sex without marriage, not to bite at back, not to disclose anyone's secrecy, pray five times a day so that you always remember your Lord and abstain from all crime and evil punch, complete 30 days fasting to revitalize your internal organs by giving special rest to your body in the sacred month of Ramazan and obtain special grace of Allah, always remember Allah to get inner satisfaction, have patience during hard days and pray more, glorify Allah more during happy moments and give thanks to Allah, follow the orders and teaching of Hazrat Muhamed (SA) practically in life. But I am a Muslim only because of my birth – practically I am a not a Muslim. My father taught my sisters how to behave and how to appear in the society and so did my mother. My father taught them that women are the diamonds and diamonds cannot be left here and there ignorant or uncovered – they must be kept in the most safe place and in proper way so that others cannot see them. My younger sister did not like to be in hijab and used to argue with my mother. My father asked her if the road is full of dust and dirty things what will you do – will you cover you feet or will you cover the road. Allah has created you women in such a way that you are special and easily all eyes be on you – so better to save yourself. Instead of covering the road cover your feet, you will not get dust. She did not dare to argue any more. My father very gently and lovingly told her that in the beginning humans were naked and Allah taught them to cover themselves. Initially they learnt to used minimum clothes and as the society progress humans learnt to use maximum clothes as a mark of civilized and progressive society. So don't try to be primitive again by wearing less clothes and don't show your body. Allah has forbidden to compare and compete with each other and not to show your wealth to others. Don't make love or show your love with your spouse in front of those who are unmarried or not getting love, don't boast of your health in front of those who are suffering from diseases, don't show your wealth in front of the poor. Always be humble and remain down-to-earth. If you cannot help people then at least don't hurt or harm them. Don't take revenge rather try to be friendly even with your enemies etc… My father used to teach us these fundamental principles of Islam being a Muslim. But I was far away from following these principles. As I was sank in the memory of past, I was feeling drowsy as if my body wanted to sleep but the severing cold didn't allow me to sleep. Last night was also a bad night for me.

All of a sudden I heard another scream – a scream of a girl. Her scream pierced through my ears. I stood up and tried to find from where it was coming. Actually it was coming from the basement of the building where I was trying to sleep. The darkness covered the night and it became darker due to the heavy dense fog. Everywhere silence prevailed except that basement. A painful cry for help and deep agony was coming through the scream. I tried to see what was going on – why was the girl crying. As I moved inside the basement of the building, I saw the guard was sleeping after drinking a lot as the liquor bottle was there. I tried to awake him but I was not able to awake him. The scream was becoming more sharp and deep as if someone groaning in deep pain. I was also afraid as I was not aware what was going on. As I went little far I saw a car standing with its dim light. Three men were torturing a short height fair girl – they tore her clothes making her almost naked, one person was busy in beating her heartlessly while other two hold her so that she cannot defend herself. I doubted they will kill her as the torture was horrible. He was kicking at her lower abdomen and punching on her body here and there. She was groaning in deep and unbearable pain helplessly. That man was saying something angrily at her –

"We have bought you and you must please our customers but you are misbehaving with our customers. Today we will give you special training how to please a man" – said that angry wolf. "Make her lie on the ground"

The scene was like a deer that was caught by three hungry wolves. The wolves were ready to tear her into pieces. If I still watch it like a deaf and dumb, they will eat her flesh alive. I quickly went to those people with whom I was sleeping and forcefully awoke them and inform the matter. Many of them rushed towards the basement. As we started moving towards the wolves and started shouting at them, they became afraid. They got into the car leaving her alone and went away at a high speed. I ran to her. Blood was coming from her mouth and nose. She was almost naked. She was a fair, beautiful and short height girl – seemed to be a Nepali. Her body bears scratching marks here and there. Oh my god! A bottle of cold drink was half inserted inside her private part. She lost consciousness. We were totally shocked to see her wretched condition. She was in need of immediate medical care. One of the labourer brought a shawl and covered her naked body. We took her to the nearby hospital. But the doctor wants police report before starting treatment. Two persons went to the police station and reported the matter. After fifteen minutes police came to see the matter. The police started interrogating us and we informed the matter to the police. I took the police to the site of crime and explained everything that I saw. The police started investigating the matter. I came back to the hospital. Almost four hours were over but still she was unconscious. The police told us to stay there. But my bag was left at that place where I was sleeping and others were also having their belongings there. So me and one labourer stayed in the hospital. Rest went to that place. I told them to take care of my bag. It was very cold but we forgot all about it and even we did not feel it at that time. After one hour the nurse told us that she has gained consciousness. I went to her but she was still afraid and not so fine. The hospital authority informed the police that she has gained conscious. The police came to take her statement. She gave her statement to the police. We all were shocked to hear her sad and pathetic story. She started to narrate her tale – "I am Layara from Nepal. I am fourteen years old. A devastating flood destroyed everything. Many villages were devastated. We lost everything. We got a shelter under a relief camp where many homeless people like us took shelter. This help was provided to us by an NGO. The food packets we got were not enough to satisfy our hunger. After three days we were staying there without food and water as the supply of food was very less. Many people were ill but there was no medical facility. What to do, where to go, How to overcome the problem – all the matters were uncertain. My younger brother was suffering from high fever. My elder sister was having health problem. We had no work to earn money. My parents were helpless. Situation was getting worst. A group of persons including some ladies came to the camp. They were offering jobs. But they were offering jobs only to 12 years to 30 years old girls and women. The job was to work in hotel or houses in Delhi or Kolkata or Mumbai or any big city. Many parents sold their daughters and many persons sold their wives.

Raju, a neighbor of us, came my father and said in sad heart –

"I got 15000 rupees for Maya. I have given her to that gentleman. He is very good. He will give her food, clothes and shelter. She will get a job in hotel."

"Shame Raju! Shame Raju! You sold your own daughter for 15000 rupees. How did you do that?" – said my mother angrily.

"What will she do with us? I cannot keep her here to die out of starvation. I don't have a home – I have nothing to feed my family. Everything is washed away by the flood. At least she will get a good life – she will have meals and shelter there. I can start a new life somewhere with this money. Once theses hard days are over I will brought her back."

"Why are you not going there for job?"

"They are not taking man. The job is for female only – working as housemaid in rich people's houses or in hotels. She will get salary, food and shelter. I think I have not done anything wrong in this situation."

My younger brother was crying as he was having high fever. He was hungry also. My mother was trying to soothe him. All remain silent for a while.

"If you want money give your daughters also. He still needs five more girls."

My parents remain silent.

"Layara you can help your family. Already Maya will be with you. You are not going alone. Many girls are going together. No need to be worried. You will get salary, food and shelter."

My parents remain silent.

"What do you think Bahadur? You will get 30000 rupees

for your two daughters. You can start a new life with that money. Your daughters will also get a good life. It is better to send them there for job than to keep here to die out of starvation."

"Ramu's wife is also going."

He kept pursuing my father. My parents remained silent and looked at each other. My elder sister got ready –

"Yes uncle we will go. You bring money. You are right if we stay here we all will die. But if we get this job our family will be saved."

"Come with me. Bahadur, you also come with me."

We went to that camp. Two ladies and two men in their nice attire seemed to be gentleman were interacting with the parents. He told my father –

"You will get 30000 rupees now. Your daughters will get salary, free food and accommodation. Your daughters will send you money every month. They will get job in hotels and in rich people's houses as maids. They will be able to live a better life and your family also."

"Can you give a job to me also." – asked my father.

"Not now – this time we need only female workers. Later I will inform you when we will be in need of male workers."

So my father agreed. Around 15 girls under 18 years age and 6 house wives under 30 years age came together for the purpose of earning money by working as maids in rich people's houses and hotels. First we came to Siliguri, a city in West Bengal, India. We stayed there in a house for 10 days. We were given nice food, clothes and beauty cosmetics. We were feeling happy. After that we were sent in small groups of 2 or 3 girls to different cities. I came to Delhi with two other girls. Here we are forced to sell our body. We are thrown in prostitution house. We have here no name and no identity. We were threatened that they will kill us if we refuse. We were bound to sell our body. We felt very bad when we understood that we are not going to get any salary as they have purchased us by paying to that crooked agents who brought us from our village by telling lie. I don't know where Maya and my sister are. They did a lot of physical torture. We cannot find any way to escape from them. Four months over! Selling my body and soul! Now I don't like to do this anymore. So I requested them to let me go home. But they gave me electric shock; sometimes they will whip me with a belt if I refuse to sell my body. I was in hell. They used to drop us to different flats or houses or hotels at night for two hours or three hours or sometime full night and pick us back to hell. There we are offering our body to the customers — sometimes to some loving gentleman, sometimes some rude middle aged man, sometimes a group of heartless men. Yesterday I was having severe pain in my lower abdomen and I told them that I cannot go tonight. But the customer had chosen me. I was forcibly sent to a room where three men were ready to enjoy me but I was not in condition to fulfill their desire. I requested them but they started laughing and taunting. I felt very bad. I had bitten one of them as I was not able to bear the pain as they were very rude. They tied my hands and legs and put clothes inside my mouth and tortured extremely for two hours one by one. I was hired for two hours and they complained to our agents that I misbehaved and did not satisfy them and that man showed the bitten mark on his hand and demanded money back. My agents became very angry on me. They started abusing me as the same complain they are receiving for last three four days. I was not feeling well at all. They told me that one more customer is there only for one hour and warned me to behave properly and to satisfy him. But I disagreed and started shouting at them. After that they stopped the car and started beating me heartlessly and the torture was unbearable. I lost consciousness. Tears rolled down from eyes. Sir please save me. Please save me from those animals."

The police took her statement and told her to calm down. They will protect her. I talked to the girl and told her how I brought her here. I felt very sad after listening her incident and felt sorry for her. It was already morning 8' clock. I have to go for my interview. I told her that I will meet her after attending interview. She thanked me a lot. My dress was not so good now. I went to a Sulabh Toilet and paid Rs 5 to get refreshed. After washing my hands, legs and face with cold water I felt relaxed. Already one of the labourers brought my bag with him in the hospital. I started moving towards that hotel where interview was going on.

Chapter - VI

I reached there on time. As usual crowd was there. Many new candidates came to attend the interview. I asked the reception counter girl when my turn will come. She asked my number and checked the list and told that it would take two more hours. I went outside to have some food. I purchased one newspaper to search job from classified advertisement. The newspaper front page had the headlines – "Delhi Girl Brutally Raped by a Gang in a Moving Bus Last Night." I was shocked. I heard her painful scream last night. It was the scream of this girl. If I were little active I could have saved her. As I read the news it gave a very brutal account of her rape. She was brutally beaten and raped by the gang in a moving bus and an iron rod was inserted in her private part. Her condition is serious.........

I felt very shocked. I came to a small restaurant for some food. There also the news of her rape was highlighted in TV as it was the main news in all media. People were expressing mixed reactions after watching the news.

"Late night the girl was roaming alone with her boyfriend! It is natural that she will be a victim of such brutal incident. How much police will protect if we are not cautious. Girls must stop roaming late night." – said one man.

"Brother these girls are leading a life beyond limit. Their

parents are careless – they have no control. They are allowing their daughters to roam in midnight. This is obvious to happen." – said another man.

"The size of dress of these girls are so small that they attracting and inviting rapists to rape them. They are roaming almost naked!" said an old man.

"Stop these nonsense! Don't blame girls like this. We must change our mentality. Search and hang these rapists in public like Saudi Arabia – see no one will dare to touch any girl against her will." said a young man.

I finished eating as I was listening to all these comments made by different people sitting in the restaurant. I opened the pages of the newspaper and saw some direct walk-in-interview ads with contact no and address. I saw one ad written "Aggressive sales man needed urgently." I planned to attend one of them after attending this interview.

I went back to the interview venue as almost two hours were over. Now my turn will come. Yes I was almost there – only after three candidates my turn will come. I managed my hair and dress to look little smarter. I forgot to wear the tie. I took it out from the bag and wore it. Mentally I was ready to face the interview. My turn came and I went inside. One gentleman was sitting in the middle and two ladies were by his side.

"Please come and sit down."

I sat on the chair kept there.

"So tell us something about you."

I started giving self introduction.

"What are your strengths?"

"Positive will power and hard work."

"What are your weak points?

I thought a while but could not find any weak point in me.

So I said –

"I don't know."

"You don't know. It means you don't have any weak points? Am I right?"

I remain silent for while.

"Why should we recruit you? How will you be beneficial for us?"

"I can do any work for you. I have good communication skills. I am good in computer operating and in managing all office related works. I can also do administrative work. I will work for you with commitment and dedication."

Meantime a servant came with water and gave me a glass of water. The man told me to drink the water. I drank and kept the glass on the table.

"Can you break that glass?"

I looked at him with surprise.

"Please break that glass."

I was surprised. I thought he is joking. He told me to go the dustbin kept in the corner. I went there. He told me to see what is inside.

"Can you see broken glasses?"

"Yes."

"We want employees who only follow our orders blindly without judging whether it is true or false. Can you follow our orders blindly?"

"I cannot follow everything blindly. But I will execute each and every order given by you."

"Can you tell me how many pieces of glass you will get if you break this glass."

I thought I am attending interview under a mad man. I felt awkward at his questions and way of asking questions.

"Yes tell us how many pieces of glass will be there if this

glass is broken."

I stood up and broke the glass on the floor and started counting the pieces of glasses. Immediately the peon came and started cleaning the floor.

"Ok Mr Sohail no need to count. Wait for our call. We will inform you interview result within a couple of days."

"Ok Sir. Thank you."

My interview was over. I came to the reception counter. Many candidates were waiting outside for their turn.

"Anything else do I need to do?"

"No sir. You may go home. We will inform you interview result within a couple of days."

I left the hotel. I was feeling relaxed but uncertain. I started moving towards the venue of another walk-in-interview advertised in the newspaper. On the way I saw a street- food-vendor was selling rajma rice. I had one plate. It was nice.

Around 3 o'clock I reached that walk-in-interview venue. Here also gathering was there but it was not that much. I went to the reception counter.

"I am a candidate for interview."

"Is your registration done sir?"

"Registartion? No It is not done."

She gave me a job application form.

"Sir fill this form and submit it with Rs 200 registration fees. After 8 candidates you can attend the interview."

"Ok Madam. I will do that."

I checked my purse only Rs 240 was left. Without thinking anything I filled the form and submitted with Rs 200."

I was waiting for my turn. After one hour my turn came. I was called inside for interview –

"May I come in sir?"

"Yes please."

I went inside. One man along with his assistant was sitting. I was offered a seat.

"Have you brought your resume."

"Yes sir."

I took out my resume from the fie and handed it over to him.

"Introduce yourself."

I started giving my introduction.

"Ok Mr Sohail. We are searching aggressive sales person for selling financial products like insurance, loan etc. Are you comfortable in marketing job?"

"Yes.. yes sir I am comfortable."

"But you don't have any experience in this field. We will provide some training. But you have to attend the training at your own cost for one week. Can you afford one week training cost?"

"How much sir?"

"It depends on you - what type of accommodation you prefer to stay and your food choice. It may be around Rs 7000 to Rs 10000."

"Yes sir I can afford."

"How will you attract customer if you have to sell a new product?"

"It depends on the situation, the products quality and demand and what type of customer I am going to deal with and what I am going to sell."

"Are you comfortable to visit customers door to door for selling your products?"

"Yes I can do that."

"Sometime you have to work under pressure and you have to fulfill target."

"I can work under pressure sir."

"If you fail to meet the target you may lose your job also."

"I will try my best to achieve the target."

"If you can deposit the training amount now, you can join us after finishing the training. Job offer will be given as soon as you deposit the training amount."

"I need one week time sir."

"Ok no problem. Be in touch with us."

He gave me a visiting card. My interview was over.

I was going towards the station. The sun was about to set and the day was going to over. Very soon the darkness of black night was going to cover the city. I was feeling tired. The road was full of traffic, the streets and markets were full of people, the buses were also full of people. I felt as if I was drowned in the ocean of people. All are in hurry. All are restless. I came to the station. The station was also over crowded. Long queues were there in front of the ticket counters. I had no intention to stand in long queue for getting the ticket. I heard the announcement of arrival of a train that was going towards my destination. But it was a superfast train and it won't give stoppage at that station where I need to get down. I went to the enquiry counter to get information of trains bound to my destination. I came to know that a train that will go to my destination was scheduled to arrive after 3 hours. I remember that I don't have enough cash to buy a ticket. I started searching for an ATM. I saw two ATMs near the station and went there. I wanted to withdraw Rs 300 but the ATM was not able to dispense Rs 300. The security guard of the ATM told me that the ATM will dispense only Rs 500 or Rs 1000 notes. But I was having balance in my bank account less than Rs 500. So I went to find other

ATMs. After trying with four ATMs I was able to withdraw Rs 300 from a SBI Bank ATM near the crossing.

I came back to the station and sat down in the waiting room. All of sudden I remembered that I had to meet that Nepali girl whom I saved last night. But I was too tired. I had limited cash. I ignored it. A man was sitting near me. He also seemed to be tired. I asked him-
"Where are you going?"
"I am going to Etawah and you?"
"I am going to Morena."
"What is your name?"
"My name is Sohail Shekh. And your name?"
"I am Ankit Dixit. I am doing job here."
"I am in search of a job. I came to attend interview here."
"How was your interview?"
"It was fine. I got selected as a sales man."
"In which company?"
"I am selected by a recruitment agency. They are recruiting for HDFC, ICICI, MAX, BAJAJ, AXIS. I have to take a short training. After that I will get the job."
"Are they asking for any money?"
"Yes I have to bear the training cost around Rs 7000 – Rs 10000."
"Brother becareful! Already I lost Rs 20000 as I was cheated by a job consultancy. It is well planned drama. They will take Rs 100 to Rs 1000 for registration and after that they will ask you to pay Rs 10000 to Rs 20000 as security deposit or training fees. Once the money is deposited you will never find there address. I became a victim of this. Please check properly before making any payment."

"Yes. I will check. I also had doubt as the interview interaction was peculiar."

"If you are interested in sales job I can help you to get a job in my company."

"It will be a great help brother if you assist me to get a job. I am interested to do any job – sales, administration, accounts, clerical etc."

"You please note down my number. I will come back Delhi after 5 days. You can come next week. I will tell details."

I noted down his number.

"What is your qualification? You must be at least high school passed."

"I have completed Graduation."

"Good! Then easily you will be selected."

"How much salary can I get?"

"Salary depends on your performance in interview. Around Rs 4500 to Rs 6000 will be your fixed salary and incentives based on your sales performance. The more you will sell the more you will earn. Even if you perform well you can become area sale manager. If you work hard you can earn well. But it is not so easy. I am planning to quit this job."

"Why?"

"I am facing family problems. Whatever I am earning its major part is spent to pay rent, electricity bill, water charges, food cost etc. Already you know that living cost in Delhi is very high. I am not able to save more. It is not beneficial anymore for me. I am not able take care of my family. Rather I am planning to start farming work in my father's farm. Here I am working hard and generating revenue for others. If I do that hard work systematically in my own farm I will get the full benefit and stability."

"But now farming is not at all profitable. Farmers are committing suicide. Its future is uncertain."

"That's a fact. But if done with proper system I am sure I can earn more than two times what I am earning by doing this job."

There was an announcement in the station and it announced about a train's arrival.

"My train is coming. Ok see you next week."

"Ok I will call you."

I was in dubious situation. Whatever he told I cannot ignore. I cannot give money to job consultancy agent. They may cheat me. I was feeling hungry. I came outside in search of a street-food-vendor but I did not find any. So I went to a cheap hotel to have my dinner. As I sat for dinner in that hotel I can watch TV. It was showing news. After 2 minutes it was showing the news that – "Delhi police special team has caught a group of flesh mongers with the help of a Nepali girl. After raiding three different places, the police has rescued 35 girls. Most of them are from Nepal, Assam, West Bengal and Bangladesh. two powerful political leaders are closely associated with the flesh mongers. Delhi gang raped victim Nirbhaya's condition is very critical." I had a simple dinner with chapatti and vegetables but had to pay two times more than street food price. I came back to the station as my train was about to come. I saw the ticket counters were not so crowd. I stand in a queue and got a ticket for my destination. Soon an announcement was made about the arrival of the train on platform no 3 and I reached there. I managed a berth in sleeper coach by paying Rs 150 to the TTE. I reached home happily as I was almost assured that

I will get a job in Delhi with the help of that man.

www.ingramcontent.com/pod-product-compliance
Lightning Source LLC
LaVergne TN
LVHW050420160726

843469LV00041B/1158